To: Marlyn

[signature]

The
Shoeshine
of Kabul

Zahra Omar Shansab

Headline Books, Inc.
Terra Alta, WV

The Shoeshine Of Kabul

by Zahra Omar Shansab

To order additional copies of this book or for book publishing
information, or to contact the author:

Headline Books, Inc.
P. O. Box 52
Terra Alta, WV 26764
www.headlinebooks.com

Tel: 304-789-3001
Email: mybook@headlinebooks.com

ISBN: 9781946664280

Library of Congress Control Number: 2018940923

To all the children whose courage and awe for life help them survive wars, hunger, illnesses and other personal hardships.

One

Malik sat down and leaned against the brick wall separating the Kabul river and the sidewalk. He gingerly placed his shoeshine box on the battered, gray asphalt. The wooden surface of the box was stained with black and brown shoe polish. A frayed rope wrapped around it, keeping the contents from falling out. Malik opened the box and neatly arranged his brush and shoe polish tin cans on the ground in front of him. He rubbed his cracked hands together and looked around.

Kabul was preoccupied with its daily hustle and bustle. Stench and a cloud of gray dust lingered overhead like a ghost threatening to suck away any breathable air still left in the city.

Peddlers shouted at the top of their voices, praising the freshness of their produce and the unbeatable prices being offered just for the day.

Out yelling one another was their preferred tactic at beating the competition and persuading shoppers to buy from them and not from the other peddlers, only a few feet away.

One peddler on Malik's right, selling the same produce as a peddler to his left, winced as he heard "five *rupias* (pennies), five rupias, lowest prices. Lowest prices guaranteed."

The peddler on the left finally raised a banana and screamed, "Free bananas, one free banana with each purchase, get your free banana."

After screaming "Free bananas" for a good minute and with no takers, he stopped to rest his irritated throat, but could still hear his neighbor screaming, "Lowest prices guaranteed." He winced and quickly took a sip of tea from a small, crusty glass.

He looked at the peddler and under his breath, muttered, "Who does he think he is? My family is dying of hunger, and this jerk is forcing me also to offer a free banana just to meet my minimum for the day. I should stuff the banana down his throat so that he would shut up."

Realizing that his frustration wasn't getting him anywhere, he looked at his rival and shouted, "Hey, brother! What's the occasion? Have you uncovered some treasure chest in your backyard before coming to work today? Is that why you can drop prices this low? How is one to make a rupia, when you pull this kind of stuff?"

But the peddler to Malik's right ignored him and continued to scream, "lowest prices guaranteed. Check around. Get the most for your money right here."

The peddler to Malik's left threw down the banana and spat out his gooey-green *naswaar* (chewing tobacco) onto the curb.

Watching the peddlers interact made Malik giggle. He witnessed this drama unravel every day, as he took his place alongside seven more young shoeshines.

Malik stared at the dry riverbed. He had never seen any water flow through it. How could the water make a path through all this garbage, he often wondered. Only a flood could move this monster of rubbish that had embedded itself into the river. He tried to visualize the murky, yellowish, floodwater rushing through the middle of the river and moving all the trash that had accumulated over the years.

But then he thought of all the little kids poking and picking through the trash who would also get swept away by the force of the raging water. They would disappear with the roar of the water, never to be seen again. The idea of such a horrific incident sent shivers down his spine. But then he realized he imagined it all. Still, he shook his head and looked at the kids playing in the riverbed.

"That would be horrible. Scary, very scary," Malik said out loud.

"What is scary?" asked Nahim, his friend who sat next to him. Malik looked at him with surprise. He had not realized he had spoken out loud.

Embarrassed, he collected his thoughts and then described his scary vision of raging water swallowing the kids.

"Don't be afraid," Nahim said, "That would never happen. My father says chances of blood flowing through this river are much higher than water." Nahim looked at the riverbed and took a deep breath. "Russians murdered so many of us. Now, foreigners are killing us once again. With everything we have endured, I am surprised blood is not already flowing through the river."

All of a sudden, Malik thought Nahim did not sound like a sixteen year old boy. He sounded more like an angry, bitter man who had failed, was frustrated and had given up.

It is hard to believe that he is only four years older than me thought Malik. He was much more like an adult. Wiser and braver than me. But also angrier and more bitter than me. Malik drifted in his thoughts and stared at Nahim with a gloomy, worried face.

Nahim recognized Malik's worried look. He was aware of Malik's mind wandering off.

"Where have you gone now?" Nahim asked.

But again, Malik was deep in thought. Nahim waved his hand and snapped his finger. "Hey!" he called out. "Do you know what a toilet is?"

"A what?" Malik asked.

"You know, a toilet," repeated Nahim. "Wealthy people have a private room inside their homes and they call it a bathroom. Unlike us, they don't have to look at everybody's crap every time they have to relieve themselves. Personally, every time I have to use the outhouse, my whole life flashes in front of me. I try not to look down at the hole in the ground. But my friend, my curiosity might just kill me one day. One day, I'll forget and look at that hole in the ground. I know, looking at it, I'll get dizzy, and before you know it, I'll fall into that stinking hole. And I'll sink deeper and deeper into a huge pile of crap. I'll try to hold on to something, but it drags me deeper and deeper. I wake up all sweaty and panicky. I don't know about you, but I get nightmares all the time about falling through that hole. I know, what you think. Scary crap, right?" Nahim laughed. "Okay, let me explain to you what a toilet is. There is this thing that looks exactly like an armchair, only without the arms and a hole in the bottom. But, you don't see the hole. You don't crouch over a hole. You sit up like on a chair, high up and away from the hole and the crap below. There is more distance between you and the hole and the pile of crap. And there is no chance of falling through a crap hole in the wobbly floor."

He stared at Malik for a second and continued. "Do you get the picture of a toilet? And when your business is done, you just pull a handle that is attached to the back of this thing, and everything gets flushed away."

Nahim remained quiet for a moment and said "So if you ask me, Kabul river is like a toilet that never gets flushed. But if we are lucky and get some powerful downpours, some of that crap might move down the river. So, you see, there is no reason to get worried about a flood through the river. I know you are a village boy and haven't lived here long enough. But don't be afraid. Don't fear the city. Besides you're with me, the Kabuli Expert!"

Malik stared at Nahim and laughed.

"You do, believe me, right?" asked Nahim.

"I believe you," said Malik with a smile. Malik felt grateful for having found Nahim, also known as the Kabuli Expert. They instantly bonded and became friends. From the day he started his new job of shining shoes, Nahim watched out for him and tried to cheer him up, whenever he was down and gloomy.

Maybe Nahim could sense how much pain and agony he felt every passing moment. "Thanks, Kabuli Expert...," Malik barely managed to get those words out. He choked up, as he often did. The thought of his village struck a painful cord again, stirring up his bitter memories of the day his village was bombed. The destruction turned it into an image of what hell might look like.

Malik's idea of hell was based on what his grandmother had always described to him. Her description of hell would usually be prompted by a slight mischief he had committed and was caught. She would warn him that he would be sent to hell if he didn't stop his numerous acts of mischief such as taking an apple from the neighbor's yard. Malik remembered that day well when he and his friends entered the neighbor's unfenced yard and picked up apples from under the apple tree. He had justified their action saying they were discarded by the tree itself. They were just laying around there on the ground and were rotting away. "Why should one let them go to waste?" he had asked his grandmother. But his furious grandmother would not listen to his reasoning.

"No!" she retorted. "That is not a reason why you should take them without permission! Let them rot, but do not dare to steal them! Understand?" She thrust her wrinkled hand forward and pointed at his face with her finger.

"But I did not take one alone!" Malik called out. "Each one of my friends took one, too!" But, before he could finish pleading his case, Malik was painfully interrupted by his ear getting twisted.

"Ouch..don't." He cried out. But his grandmother did not let go of his ear.

"Grandmother," pleaded Malik, as he looked at her stern face.

"Don't be such a naughty boy," warned his grandmother. "Do you understand that it's a sin to talk back to grownups. Especially to your grandmother?"

Malik nodded sheepishly but wondered why he was always too slow to react and not fast enough to escape her clutches. Why was he still surprised since it happened all the time? He resolved to be quicker next time and slip away before his next ear twisting session. *Besides, why get one's ear twisted, when a scolding is enough*, he thought. It hurt badly. Either Grandmother was too clever and slick, or he was too slow and stupid.

His mother always called him gullible. *Maybe that was my problem*, he thought.

Nevertheless, his grandmother's description of hell always terrified him. She would describe to him how hell was divided into different chambers that were assigned to different sins.

Malik immediately pictured himself banished to the "Apple Thieves" chamber where he would surely notice some familiar faces. Oh, yes, the faces belong to my friends getting punished in hell for the same crime. He smiled, *at least I won't be alone there!*

But that comforting thought vanished when his grandmother proceeded to describe how the fires of hell would engulf all sinners and burn them down to ashes. She would continue describing the scorching heat of hell and how painful it would feel. By the end of the lecture, Malik remembered how bitter his mouth had tasted and how much he regretted eating that half-rotten apple.

Two

On that unfortunate day, when the planes appeared in the sky over his village, he witnessed hell. Hearing the loud noises of the aircraft, he felt something terrible was about to happen. For the past few weeks, he had overheard the conversations of the grownups sitting in the shadow of the tall mud walls surrounding the village. He heard something about foreigners getting ready to invade Afghanistan. They were looking for Osama who apparently was hiding somewhere in a cave. Malik did not know who Osama was, and quite frankly, he did not even care who he was and into which cave he had crawled. He had enough troubles of his own and was still disturbed by the hellish tale prompted by that cursed apple he had taken, or according to his grandmother, stolen.

When deafening sounds of the planes got close, he ran towards his family's mud hut. He didn't know why he was running but was confident his father would protect him from these monsters chasing him. His heart was beating very fast as if it wanted to cut open his chest and break free like a frightened bird from a cage. His knees were wobbly, causing him to trip and fall. He crawled for a few seconds before he could get up and run again. Not too long after he was running again, a loud explosion knocked him off his feet. And as he fell, he caught a glimpse of what seemed like a red dragon spitting fire.

It swallowed up several huts one after the other with an insatiable hunger. It seemed like a beast twirling and twitching, and it lurked forward leaving behind a trail of ashes and smoke and ear-piercing screams. The shock of the scene robbed Malik of his willpower. He sat on the ground, frozen with fear and disbelief. Once again, he tried to get back on his feet, but could only crawl. The deafening sounds of explosions grew closer and louder. Cold sweat trickled down the back of his neck. He struggled to his feet. The fumes, dust, and smoke invaded his senses. "What is going on *Khoda jan* (dear God)?" he cried out loudly.

"What is going on?" he asked again sobbing, as villagers ran by him dragging their children behind them.

Everyone was running to save their loved ones from the bombs which were quickly reducing their village to a graveyard.

Overcome by panic, Malik got up again and ran. Maybe this is a nightmare. *I know everything will be fine once I wake up*, he thought. *If this is the punishment for stealing that rotten apple, I promise never to take apples from the neighbor's garden again! I promise Khoda jan! I promise! Toba (forgive me, God).*

Either God was not listening, or it was not about stealing apples. The explosions continued and the cries and blood-curdling screams went on. After what felt like an eternity, Malik finally reached his hut. But as he pushed the door open, his father grabbed him by his arm and pushed him back out the door.

In his other arm, his father was holding his younger sister. His mother was crying and trying to cover her face with her *chador* (head scarf). "What are you doing, son?" his father yelled. "Run, we are following right behind." He then gave Malik another push forcing him to run.

Malik remembered running, running very fast and every few seconds he would turn around to make sure his family was following behind. He remembered seeing everyone taking off towards the mountains. The next thing he recalled was sitting underneath a rock. Trembling with fear, he was unable to realize what kind of disaster had just struck them. His ears felt as if they were stuffed with dirt; everything sounded muffled.

He looked around and saw hundreds of villagers taking shelter behind the rocks. Women and children were crying. Some women beating their chest in agony. Malik wondered, *is this hell?*

Three

"*Malik Agha* (sir), what is going on?" the voice of Nahim transported him back to the side of Kabul river.

"What is hell?" asked Malik, without realizing why he said that.

"What do you mean?" Nahim asked. "I hope you are not planning a trip there,"

Nahim smirked. "You don't have to waste your time traveling there my friend," he said. "You are already there." His smile widened, "Kabul has turned into one. Explosions, hunger, death, homelessness is right here and poor people like you and me suffer every day." Nahim paused and stared into the far distance, a frown covering his face. He stayed frozen like that for a good while, appearing lost in deep thought.

Finally, he jumped to his feet, shook his head and then bent down to look into Malik's face. He looked at Malik with a stern gaze but then smiled and winked at him. "But let me point out a difference my friend, at least God will not discriminate between rich and poor when we are judged. But here my friend, we suffer every day, and our biggest sin is our poverty. For that, we are punished every day."

Nahim did not sound like a teenager, Malik thought. *He sounded more like the angry old men he had heard talking in the bazaar.* But then, some of the older shoeshine boys would also speak like Nahim whenever they were frustrated or didn't make enough money to buy bread for their siblings waiting at home.

Malik regretted asking Nahim about hell. He felt guilty for making his friend pensive. Trying to sound light-hearted, he yelled out to Nahim,

"Hey, at least if we do end up in hell, it won't be such a shock."

"Damn right!" yelled back Nahim and they laughed.

That day work was very slow. Malik polished few pairs of shoes. He did not make much money and at one point, a tall, bearded man yelled at him for skimping on shoe polish.

The man told Malik he wasn't doing a good job and threw the change in his face. Angrily, he walked off huffing and puffing.

Of course, Malik had to be careful with how much polish he used, but he never did a bad job. He always tried to do his best but sometimes his customers would take their daily frustrations out on him.

A loud bicycle horn startled Malik. He whirled his head in its direction. A man, cycling past pedestrians disappeared in the distance. He heard the bicycle horn a couple more times, but the sound faded as he rode away. The bicyclist also became smaller and smaller and soon just appeared like a small dot.

Malik saw that the sun was beginning to descend behind a thick cloud of dust. He followed the dimming rays of the sun onto the riverbed and noticed a strange reflection coming from a small puddle. He looked closer, but couldn't make out what was reflecting so brightly from the river. *Definitely not the scales of a fish,* he thought.

Fish live in the water, not in a pile of trash. He tried to focus harder by squinting his eyes. Then, a big smile spread across his face, when he realized he had solved the puzzle. "A can of Cacola," he shouted, grinning ear to ear. Loud laughter broke out right next to him. Malik turned around and found Nahim laying on his back laughing loudly.

Still laughing, Nahim said, "You are too funny when you talk to yourself! What did you just say? Cacola? It is not…," but before he could finish his sentence, another burst of laughter seized his frail body.

"Well, Mr. *Dehaati* (villager), it is Co…ca… co…la," Nahim pronounced precisely.

"Fine, Mr. Expert," Malik said, "That's enough making fun of me!" Malik made a fist and shook it at Nahim while trying to look mean.

"You need to learn these things and possibly a few more *Angrezi* (English) words. Do you see all those yellow-haired foreigners and soldiers all over the city?" Before waiting for an answer, he went on. "They are changing Kabul. This will be a different city soon," he smiled, "We may even get to polish some boots one day and get paid in dollars. You should try and learn certain things. They will help you survive."

As Malik listened to Nahim, the words 'boots, soldiers, foreigners' started to ring in his ears over and over again. Nahim's voice soon faded away, and he felt himself slowly drown into the cold, dark abyss of his past. He tried to resist and free himself from his memories. But their grasp was firm and merciless. It kept dragging him deeper and deeper. Once again, he inhaled the fumes, smelled the fire and heard the cries. He saw himself trying to run, but he stood still as if frozen in time. He tried to scream, but he had lost his voice. His face was wet, but he was not crying. He felt warm blood oozing somewhere on his face. He looked down expecting to see his patched-up shoes, but he gasped in fear. On his feet was a pair of canvas boots that were being covered by blood dripping from his face. Terrified, he tried to get the boots off by kicking his feet. He started to scream. "Get off of me you bloody boots! Get off of me!"

"Hey, what is going on?" yelled Nahim. "Calm down! Have you gone mad? Stop kicking and screaming! You are ruining your box. Stop it I said! What is wrong with you? Are you possessed by a *Jinn* (a spirit) or something?"

Malik opened his eyes and saw Nahim sitting on his chest, pinning down his arms to the ground. To make things even more embarrassing, they were surrounded by curious faces, mumbling, whispering. An old man wearing a dirty turban started saying a loud prayer, while another offered to take off his shoe and hold it to Malik's nose. That was a common practice for attempting to distract and help someone suffering an epileptic seizure. Malik thought he could hear many in the crowd whisper; "epileptic kid," "crazy boy." The thought of sniffing the stinky shoe of a stranger made Malik quickly sit up. He felt embarrassed and his body was hot and clammy. His stomach churned and his mouth tasted awful.

Sensing Malik's embarrassment, Nahim got up and faced the crowd of onlookers. As if to prepare for an important speech, he cleared his throat, pushed out his chest and took on a tall and proud posture.

"Dear folks," he began. "This is an obvious and sad case of how smelling shoe polish for long hours can affect the brain. That is what you just witnessed with this poor boy. So please, do not underestimate the dangerous fumes we inhale every day while polishing your shoes, prolonging the life of your shoes while shortening ours. It does take a toll on our health. So next time you get your shoes polished, please remember this and give us a good tip. And now be gone! Disperse! The show is over! If you stay another minute, you will have to pay. Now get lost!"

Most onlookers still seemed concerned, some shook their heads, others started to walk away cursing under their breaths. As the last person walked away, Nahim turned to Malik and said, "As far as you are concerned, my crazy friend, please, from now on, try not to unleash your wild side here at work. We have a reputation to worry about. If this happens again and the word gets around, no one will come to you, and you won't make a rupia anymore. Customers will be afraid you might shove the brush down their throats, instead of polishing their shoes. Alright, it's getting dark. Time to wrap up for the day. Let me help you pack up and let's go home."

Malik looked sheepishly at Nahim and stood up. Once again, he thought of Nahim being so much more mature, and wiser than him. Nahim was the sole breadwinner of his family and took care of his younger siblings and his mother. Almost all of the shoeshines sitting in that long line along Kabul river shared the same fate of being sole breadwinners.

Malik felt guilty. His friend had enough of his own problems to tackle, and now he was creating more trouble for him. "Please forgive me for making such a spectacle today! Hope you will still sit next to me tomorrow." He extended his hand, stained by black and brown polish.

Nahim shook his hand with his equally filthy and cracked hand and flushed a tired smile at Malik.

The two separated, each walking towards their destination. Relieved that his friendship was still intact, Malik took weary steps toward the ruins that he called home. His home consisted of three half collapsed walls slightly taller than him and a missing roof that had been replaced by a thick, clear plastic tarp. With each step, Malik felt more apprehensive and nervous. He tried to distract himself by entertaining the thought of buying a couple of warm and tasty flatbreads from the bakery.

The sun was almost behind the mountains. Through the thick cloud of dust and pollution, the sun appeared more like a flickering kerosene lamp surrounded by a black halo. "You must be tired too," mumbled Malik while looking at the sun. "Thank you for keeping me warm and shining on the shoes I polished today. You made my work shine."

As usual, there was a long queue at the bakery. Some wanted to buy bread and others were waiting to get their home-made dough baked in the bakery's *tandoor* (clay oven). The aroma of freshly baked bread enticed Malik's senses and he thought how much he loved and enjoyed the smell.

All of a sudden, he found himself in that lively, beautiful family hut, watching his mother kneading the dough while humming a song. Malik and his little sister followed every move of her hand with awe and admiration.

"Put some more wood in the tandoor, dear," his mother said.

Like a solder obeying his commander, Malik hopped to his feet, picked up some pieces of wood, marched to the tandoor oven and deposited the wood through its round opening.

He then proudly announced, "It is ready, Mother." He sat back down by the side of the tandoor that breathed warm air on him. The gentle warm air coming from the flames below caressed his rough cheeks. He watched his mother bring over the tray with the dough. The dough was now rolled into a few small balls.

"When will it be ready?" Malik asked his mother impatiently. His stomach rumbled in anticipation of a delicious piece of warm bread.

"What would be ready?" a voice growled at him. "The bread?" the voice continued.

"You have been waiting in this line for only twenty minutes, while I have been feeling my old legs go numb for the past hour. You must either be out of your mind or dreaming with your eyes wide open."

"Oh, not again...," Malik snapped back to the present. "No, sir. I was just wondering if *your* order was ready...but...never mind, sorry." The old man looked at him suspiciously, muttered something under his breath and then caught a glimpse of Malik's stained hands with black and brown shoe polish.

Malik noticed the man's glare at his hands. Embarrassed, he tried to hide them behind his box. For the rest of the hour he waited in line, he tried hard to keep the ghosts of the past far away. He tried not to lose himself in his thoughts and paid attention to the comments and conversations being exchanged among the waiting customers.

"...As I was saying," said a bearded man, "Karzai is an impotent president, my brother.

His people are being bombarded every day, and he is just lying down at the foreigners' feet kissing them."

"What do you expect from a puppet, brother?" said another one wearing a turban. "We got kicked out of Pakistan and Iran because Karzai made false promises to take care of our refugees, invited them to the warm and welcoming arms of the motherland, and when they got here what did they get? Hunger, plastic tents, diseases and faced by a land that is still drenched in blood!"

An angry looking man, who had been listening, with a frown on his face interrupted the turban-wearing person. "People like you make me sick to my stomach," he said. "We are the ones who suffered and are still suffering by not leaving our country. While cowards like you deserted their country and left it like a half-dead body. Left it to a slow death and for the wolves to feast on." He turned around and spat on the ground and said, "You make me sick."

The bearded man looked at him with anger and resentment as he yelled, "Nobody was holding you back! No one invited you to stay behind. We risked our lives too by crossing the bloody terrain. We tried to save our families and give them a better chance at life. Your children are your first responsibility, then comes the rest of the motherland. And besides, what did we find waiting for us on the other side, across the border? Misery, poverty, humiliation! Now listen to me! It's people like you make *me* sick to think that I have suffered as much if not more than you and then have to listen to your crap back in my own country. I can't believe we are still getting treated like refugees. The wolves, as you named the Russians, would not be able to walk away with chunks of flesh, if people like you did more to guard this country than to point fingers at others. To hell with you all!" screamed the old man.

He looked at his opponent with a fierce, threatening stare. His opponent quickly blinked and lowered his head. The old, bearded man stepped out of the line and disgustedly, he stormed off.

No one spoke. Everyone waiting in line was silent. The only voice was the baker calling out "next."

Malik just stood there and watched all this unravel with his mouth open. He had expected the situation to turn into a fist fight with people rolling in mud, blood gushing from their noses, ripped shirts and lots of black eyes. Just like an Indian movie he had once seen where the hero had tackled five villains, punishing them with mid-air kicks in the groin and knock-out punches to their heads. *Would have been entertaining*, he thought. But I guess people are too tired and hopeless to put up a fist fight this late in the day. After his long wait, he got his two pieces of flatbread.

Malik continued his walk toward the ruins where he lived. He took slow and hesitant steps, stopping now and then to stare at shop windows, to listen to a song playing on a distant radio or to watch a street vendor fry his 'jilabi' sweets. Stopping to watch the curbside candy vendor prepare his sweets was his favorite stop. He loved to see the candy maker pour the sweet white sauce for the *Jilabi*, a mixture of sugar, flour and other spices onto the hot and sizzling frying pan. He observed as the candy maker deep fried the sweet sauce and twist it into beautiful, round, honey-colored shapes.

It was like observing a master at his craft. He smelled the sweet aroma he loved so much. It felt so good to take in that particular smell that it was hard for him to walk away from it. And when he did walk away, he could smell that aroma follow him for a good while teasing his senses.

Halfway home, Malik found a plastic water bottle lying on the sidewalk. He kicked it to the opposite side of the curb. He stopped to take a look around. The bazaar was being lit by faint light bulbs and blackened kerosene lamps flickered on top of fruit and vegetable carts.

He felt an eerie sadness in that dimly lit place. Watching the dark, lonely figures of passersby made him wonder if they also felt fear and hopelessness. He tried to look into their faces for any of those signs. It was hard to study their faces. They were all rushing to get home. But the light would sometimes catch the faces, reflecting them with what appeared to be a pale, round halo. This pale halo revealed a kind of fear in their faces. Women rushed by with their children running behind them holding tightly to their mothers' green or blue *burqas* (full face and body covering outer garment). Some kids were keeping up with their mothers, others looked panicked and afraid of being left behind.

Every once in a while, a mother would let her hand emerge from underneath the burqa to gently navigate a shrieking kid in front of her. Completely covered under that monstrous piece of garment, she looked like a floating ghost.

What if a kid begins to follow the wrong mother? Malik wondered. Under the burqa all the women looked the same. No wonder the kids were freaking out. Perhaps they look at the women's shoes to make sure they are following their mothers. *This does not seem like an easy task*, Malik thought. *Maybe they are following a scent, the smell of their mother, like some baby animals do. Maybe it is something else.* Malik got tired of wondering, turned around and continued to walk toward his destination.

But with every step forward, he felt anxious and could sense his nightly fears creep into him. His heart began to pump faster, his palms sweated even though it was getting very cold. He began to feel the cold air penetrate through the little holes in his tattered shirt, making him shiver. He felt very apprehensive. His chest felt tight as if some invisible force was draining the life out of him. In an attempt to fill his lungs with air, he opened his mouth, but a shrill scream escaped from it. The loud shriek came out so suddenly as if it had been fighting for months to free itself from where it was trapped.

Panicking and self-conscious, Malik quickly looked around to make sure no one had heard him. Realizing his legs were not cooperating anymore, he sat on the window ledge of a pastry shop. *I'll take a small break and then continue*, he thought.

The aroma of baked goods made him hungry. I am starving, he thought. He turned his back to the window of the pastry shop to avoid facing the deliciously tempting, golden colored pastries. The artfully designed, flower shaped cookies, the square slices of walnut covered cake had enchanted him in an instant. He knew the exact location of each pastry behind the window. Passing by this shop every evening and staring at the display window had created a map in his memory. He could easily tell what cookies were arranged on which shelf without even glancing at the window. As he sat there, he recalled the first time Nahim proudly stood in front of this shop and gave it a very impressive introduction. He had talked about this shop as it was his own.

"You see, I know each and every cookie. I have stared at them for so long that I can practically taste them. Those with the green stuff are the pistachio ones, and the ones on that yellow tray...," he paused and squinted very hard to see the pastry more clearly. He pressed his forehead against the window to catch a closer look. At that moment, the fat, red-bearded baker jumped out of the shop and yelled at Nahim with a thin voice:

"Get your filthy face and hands off my window!"

Malik struggled not to burst out laughing. The baker's large, strong physique did not match his thin, high-pitched voice. His huge belly jiggled whenever he moved and his henna colored beard had turned out too red. *Must have left the henna for too long*, Malik thought. "I am sorry, Uncle," Nahim said, "I did not mean to rub my nose on the window, but the cookies look so good..."

Before he could finish, the baker screamed at him, "Get out of here! You filthy beggar. I watch you every day passing by my shop staring and paying a little too much attention. Do you think I don't know what you are up to? You are looking for an opportunity to steal. You filthy thief! Now buzz off before I kick your ass and shove that shoe polish down your throat."

Stunned by the man's outburst, Nahim's face turned white. He couldn't believe the abusive words hurled at him. His lips quivered and he clenched his fists.

Punch him in the nose, Malik thought. *Give him what he deserves.* But Nahim stood there, frozen in shock and anger. As the baker continued to insult and abuse him, Malik felt humiliated for his friend. Nahim also couldn't bear this humiliation any longer. All of a sudden, he felt a dark cloud hover over his face. His pulse throbbed harder through his temples. He balled his fingers into a fist. Before the baker could hurl another nasty word, Nahim roared like a wounded animal, in a voice that did not sound like him.

"Stop it you son of a bitch!" he yelled. "How dare you accuse me of being a thief? I would rather die of hunger than to steal. I spit on your cookies and those stale cakes. And yes, I was looking inside, but do you know why I was looking, you lousy liar? Half of those cookies are not even baked by you, you fraud. You just open those cookie packages brought here by the foreigners! You just arrange them on the trays, display them on the shelves, and sell them as your fresh-baked cookies. Then you boast about your fabulous recipes and that fresh flour imported from Pakistan. I know what they look like. A soldier gave me a pack once!" Nahim was so upset that he did not even stop to take a breath as he yelled at the baker.

By now, the baker was equally in a state of shock. He did not expect a retaliation and embarrassing accusations coming from a dirty, poor shoeshine.

Malik stood there speechless, not knowing how to help his friend who was consumed by rage. Malik did not like confrontations and was still unaccustomed to the ways of the city. He sheepishly looked around and noticed a big crowd had gathered to see what the commotion was all about. This was typical of the crowds who would always gather like a swarm of flies, whenever there was an argument, a fight, or just a new Bollywood song playing on someone's radio.

Malik began to imagine each face in the crowd attached to the body of a fly with gigantic wings and beady, shiny eyes that were mesmerized by a piece of candy. *Wow! That would be really funny*, Malik thought. But his imagination was disrupted by Nahim saying, "Yes! My friend right here..." Malik was yanked by his arm and shoved in front of the crowd. He looked meekly at all the faces now staring at him with curiosity and impatience. Malik wondered how much of the drama he had missed while he got lost in his fantasy. But the probing eyes of the crowd made him feel sick to his stomach.

"Go ahead tell them I am right," Nahim whispered to him.

He looked at Nahim with confusion, "What do…"

But before he could finish, Nahim hissed at him saying, "Stupid, moron…just say yes! Where have you been? In dreamland again? Have you not been listening?" Nahim cleared his throat and continued in a loud and assertive voice to the baker. "I was telling this liar that half of those foreign cookies are probably made with pork oil!" He faced Malik and asked, "Didn't your uncle say so? His uncle can read English, so tell them that those are the cookies!"

But Malik just stared at him dumbfounded. Nahim pinched his arm slightly then whispered to him again, "Now don't tell them you don't have an uncle."

Malik took a step forward, looked at the crowd and then at the baker. "Yes…., he is right, those cookies are 'haram' (not kosher to eat)." As soon as he said that, he quickly glanced at Nahim, to see if he was pleased with his performance. At the same time, he felt guilty for lying. But the baker deserved it. *We are not all thieves*, he thought, trying to justify his lie.

The baker's face was now as red as his beard. He looked guilty and felt the crowd's accusing eyes focused on him. He could hear mumblings and comments being exchanged.

All of a sudden, the baker charged towards Nahim waving his fists and shouting with his shrill voice, "I'm going to kill you, you useless liar. You are trying to ruin my business and reputation." The baker bent down to take off his shoe.

Seizing the opportunity, Nahim grabbed Malik's arm and yelled, "Run! Malik, run!"

Before the baker's flying shoe could hit them, they began to run as fast as their worn out shoes would allow. While running, Nahim continued to scream at the top of his voice, "Don't eat his haram cookies, don't eat his haram cookies."

After a few minutes of giving chase, the baker gave up. He stopped breathless, threw a couple of rocks at them and then cursed them some more.

Nahim and Malik ran for another ten minutes before pausing to take a breather. "Did...you...see... his face," Nahim asked as he gasped for air between each word. "Called me a thief," he continued, "that dishonest pig. I didn't mean for all this to happen; I just happened to notice those cookie boxes. I didn't lie and I didn't realize I had gotten so close to his dirty window! You know, Malik, I am tired of people treating us like dirty, flea-infested dogs!" He gestured to Malik to keep on moving. "Come, let's find a safe spot before that red-bearded monster comes looking for us. He is afraid to leave his shop unattended. Otherwise, he would be on our trail like a blood-sniffing hound."

Malik silently followed him, and now they were far away from the bazaar. They reached a narrow, dusty alley that led up to a few homes. "Well, thank God we are safe now," Malik said looking relieved. "All he had to do was yell 'thieves,' and the whole bazaar would have been after us. We would be black and blue after a real good beating." His face then became excited, when he remembered his determination not to get caught. "Did you see how fast I was running? I took off like lightning and all I could hear was the wind. I was running so fast that my cheeks were burning, my throat was awfully dry, and my shoes were about to rip into a thousand pieces. But I kept on running and kept looking at my big toe sticking out of this hole," Malik pointed to his shoe. "I am surprised the rest of my toes are not sticking out by now!"

As Malik followed Nahim into the alley, he kept on talking to cover up the silence. Malik sensed that his friend's feelings were badly hurt and that he felt humiliated by the incident.

Nahim did not speak and continued to walk with his head hung low.

Malik felt sorry for him, and he tried to mask his awkward silence by making fun of his shoes again. "You see we polish shoes all day long. We get to see all different kinds of shoes, different colors, different styles, stinky shoes, sweaty shoes, and oh, I hate the ones worn without socks; they are extra smelly and slippery…ewww!" Malik made a disgusted facial expression that he thought was quite funny, but Nahim did not even look at him. Not giving up, Malik continued, "I sometimes dream of running away with a pair of shoes that I really like. Some nice foreign brand. It's not worth risking your neck for cheap, fake leather ones, you know. Now, I can tell a fake one, just by looking at it. I can tell right away. You have taught me well, Master."

Nahim continued walking in silence and deep in thought. His shoulders were slumped and his head still hung low. Looking at his friend, Malik felt sad.

He felt guilty for not sticking up for him in front of the crowd, for not screaming at the baker, for not waving his fists, and not beating him like one of those movie heroes he had seen on a TV outside a video store. A movie hero would have grabbed the baker by the collar, dragged him around and thrown him at his friend's feet to make an apology. Of course before that, he would have slapped, punched and kicked him in all the right places.

I wish I could have done that to that fat, red-bearded slob, Malik thought. He went on to imagine how the crowd would have applauded, cheered and thrown kisses at him. *But I do hate fights*, he thought.

"Let's sit here for a minute," Nahim's voice brought him to a halt. He looked around and found himself at the end of a narrow alley. He glanced up and saw the tall exterior walls of some mud houses overlooking the alley. There were also some small, green painted windows facing the street. The windows seemed more like eyes watching every passerby from afar.

They sat down on the ground leaning against the wall. There were few pedestrians in the alley, only some dusty looking young children with runny noses and dirty, matted hair. Some of the children were missing pants, and they were all so covered in dirt that one could mistake them for life-sized statues formed out of clay. Mud statues with small, curious eyes and happy-go-lucky souls. Some of the children walking by looked at Malik and Nahim with curiosity. Others just flashed toothless smiles at them. Some children, lugging heavy water buckets to their homes, seemed tired and did not notice Malik or Nahim at all. Looking down at the ground in front of them, those children would stop every few feet, put down their buckets and rub the palms of their hands together to gather up the strength to continue carrying their heavy load.

Malik looked at Nahim over his shoulder and said, "You are such a fast runner! From now on, I will call you Kabuli Lightening. And also a genius for calling him out about his fake fresh cookies."

Nahim looked at him from the corner of his eyes. "No matter how fast I run, I can never outrun my destiny," he said. "It is always a few steps ahead of me. I am tired, very tired Malik. Earlier, when you were talking about which shoes you would choose to run away in, do you know what I dream when I polish them?"

Malik shook his head but was surprised Nahim, despite appearing detached, had paid attention to what he had said earlier.

Nahim continued, "I dream of a magical pair of shoes that would help me run away from this hell. A pair that would lead me to somewhere better than here. I am only sixteen. My shoulders are tired of carrying all these responsibilities. Every time I shine a pair of shoes, I shine them so well that they sparkle. Then I think maybe these are the ones with those magical powers. Sometimes, I feel the urge to leap up and run with those shoes. I dream that once I run with them, they will lift me up like the wind and help me get far, far away. To somewhere, where there is always happiness, where there is food. And no explosions, no scattered, bloody-body parts."

Nahim looked at Malik. He noticed Malik seemed frightened and nervous. "Hey, are you okay?" asked Nahim.

Malik looked at him in a bizarre way and repeated Nahim's last few words, in the exact order as if to mimic him "no scattered, bloody-body parts."

Nahim felt bad he had scared Malik with his words. He always wondered about Malik's state of mind, ever since he had gotten to know him almost a year ago. Malik never talked about his family. All Nahim knew was that Malik was forced to leave his village and move to Kabul after the village was bombed and destroyed.

Early on, Nahim had decided not to pry into Malik's life, or force him to share his past if he didn't want to. *He must have been through a lot already*, thought Nahim. *That is why he always acts so bizarre and talks to himself.*

Malik's continuing blank stare worried Nahim. Malik looked transfixed like he was looking at a ghost from the past. Nahim felt guilty for sharing his bottled up feelings with him. Never before, had he talked about his anguished feelings in his friend's presence, who had never heard this dark side of him. He had only known the funny, brave and strong Nahim. He wondered what it would take to snap Malik from his trance.

He gently nudged Malik with his elbow and with a funny voice said, "Now look here, boy! Don't you turn into a parrot on me!" But Malik did not acknowledge him. Then, pretending he had noticed something on Malik's face, Nahim said with a shocked voice, "Hey, your nose is changing. Oh no! My God! Your color is changing too. You are turning green, just look at your hands. Look, feathers are beginning to poke out from underneath your skin!" When Malik finally glanced at his hands, Nahim gently smacked the back of his head and said in a shrill voice imitating a parrot, "Fooled you, parrot boy! Come on now, let's get up and get going!"

"Very funny!" said Malik. "Now you are the one who is acting like a parrot," Malik continued, "Wait, I will capture you, cut your beautiful wings and throw you in a cage! Then I will teach you to sing a song, place you on a stand in the middle of the bazaar, and make loads of money by presenting you as an animal act. And, I will call it the Parrot with the Golden Voice Show."

With that, Malik reached to grab Nahim's arm, but Nahim pulled himself away and yelled, "No! It would be the Parrot with The Iron Claws Show! And beware Malik. You are about to lose your ever dreaming eyes to my iron claws, my friend."

Malik jumped to his feet and took off running in a hurry. Nahim pretended to be clawing at him with his calloused, cracked fingers still dirty with shoe polish.

They ran back down the same alley, and a cloud of white dust followed them from behind. But this time, they were laughing out loud, and their laughter echoed off the tall, battered mud walls.

Four

"No! I found it first! Give it back to me, you rascal!" The voice made Malik look up. He found himself still sitting in front of the pastry shop. He had lost track of time, *how long have I been sitting here*, he wondered.

"No! I found it first you liar!" said the other voice. Mailk looked at the direction of the voices and noticed two little boys not older than six, both dressed in ragged shirts, shaved heads, crusty faces, and one of them oozing a greenish discharge from his eye.

They both were holding on to an empty, plastic water bottle, exchanging dirty looks and every now and then, tugging at it. Each one had a half-full sack of empty water bottles on the ground next to him. "I'll kill you! Let it go, it's mine!" said one.

"I saw it first!" said the one with the oozing eye. "You cheat! May God strike you with lightning and split you in half for lying! Aren't you ashamed of stealing from a child?"

"How old do I look?" asked the other one. "Your grandfather's age? You are probably older than me, you crazy dog! Let go before I break your nose. This is my territory, and I collect junk from this section of the bazaar. You have crossed the line collecting junk from my turf."

"Who are you to set boundaries in the bazaar?" protested the one with the sick eye. "Who gave this section to you as a gift? Your mother? And leave my grandfather out of this!"

"Get lost you one-eyed beast! Unless you want something oozing out from your mouth too!" screamed the other boy.

Before the other child could say anything further, Malik sprang to his feet and yelled, "Stop it, you two! No reason to kill each other over a piece of junk! Here, one of you can have mine." Malik held out a plastic bottle in front of them as they stared in disbelief. The boy with the oozing eye finally let go of the bottle, and the other one quickly pulled it away and stuffed it in his sack. Malik nodded at the boy with the sick eye, who approached hesitantly, taking small steps.

"Hurry up!" said Malik with a reassuring voice. " Here, I will leave it on the ground. Come, I am not going to bite you!"

The little boy had the look of a frightened puppy, thought Malik. He kept approaching slowly, not trusting Malik, yet eager to bag the bottle. Malik realized that picking and selling junk was as special to those boys, as polishing shoes was to him. It was their livelihood. After quickly grabbing the bottle from the ground and throwing it in his sack, the boy ran away fast, using all the power in his thin body.

He stopped after a good distance making sure no one was following him. He then waved at Malik and shouted, "Thank you!" Then, he looked at his rival and yelled, "I piss on your border! I'll piss so much that you will float all the way to Russia, where they will change your name to Ivan and call you comrade!" He took off running and began to laugh out loud.

The other boy, swore under his breath, picked up his sack and went the other way.

Once again, Malik felt the chilly air sneak in through the holes of his shirt. He braced himself, rubbed his arms, then picked up the wooden box with the bread on top. He wrapped the bread with a cloth to keep it warm and started again towards his destination.

Five

The chaos of the bazaar had died down a little, and the stores were getting ready to close. Malik passed the butcher's shop and watched the butcher remove chunks of meat from the hooks and take it inside. The butcher's young assistant was scrubbing the counter with a sponge, trying to get rid of the blood stains from the sale of bloody, raw meat. The sight of blood nauseated him, and he quickly looked away.

In another shop, he noticed a pair of hands cleaning kabob skewers and putting them aside. The smell of grilled kabob still lingered in the air. The flames of the grill were dying down, flickering faintly. Malik looked closer and thought the smoldering pieces of charcoal appeared to be the red, beady eyes of a little creature trapped under the weight of the ashes, breathing slower and slower, its eyes flickering fainter and fainter.

The appetizing aroma of kabob reminded Malik that he had not eaten all day. He reached into his carefully wrapped up bread and tore a piece. It tasted really good, and he savored every bite. He tried to stop himself from tearing up another piece, but could not resist, and treated himself to a second piece of delicious, warm bread. Soon, one whole bread was gone.

Malik continued walking past the peddlers who were packing up for the evening. The blaring music from their radios was now silent. It was getting dark, and everyone was hurrying to get home. With darkness also descended a sense of fear. *Everyone seems afraid at night, not just me,* Malik thought.

He started to hurry too, and he took quick, long steps. He remembered the previous night on his way home, when a soldier had grabbed him by his sleeve, pinned him against the wall and opened his wooden box. The soldier searched through the box carefully and with suspicion. Frustrated by not finding anything of interest, he slapped Malik hard across the face and shoved him onto the sidewalk. Finally, he uttered a few curses and yelled at Malik to run home before he would throw him in jail.

Malik broke out in a cold sweat as he started to run. He ran fast, very fast, nothing stopped him. Even the painful, constant friction between his knees and the shoe shine box did not slow him down. He drew strange glances from passersby, some of whom cursed when they were accidentally bumped by him. The evening wind started to burn Malik's cheeks and the holes in his shoes caused his toes to be stung by the rough sidewalk. He could feel an occasional splinter or pebble piercing through his already cracked feet. But he kept running until he came to a complete halt in front of the ruins of a schoolhouse where he lived. The night had fully descended over the city by now, covering everything in a black veil. The school compound in which he lived, consisted of collapsed walls that once divided the classrooms. Explosions had completely blown off the roof, but most of the walls were still half standing. The half-collapsed building resembled the spirit of the city, shattered, broken, but still standing, hoping to pick up the pieces and to postpone another inevitable collapse.

At present, the ruins housed dozens of refugee families who had either returned willingly or were forced to come back from neighboring countries. Some, like Malik, had fled the violence that had destroyed their villages. Most of the people from his village lived here too.

Every corner of the building was occupied by a family. Torn, shredded tarps along with thick plastic sheets served as makeshift roofs. They were anchored down by ropes, tied to thick wooden poles and dug deep into the ground.

There was always loud, chaotic noise mixed with screams of young children running loose and playing in the dirt. The older children were all working, either carrying water or collecting junk to be resold. Women were either screaming at the kids or trying to light stoves with broken tree branches. They would hustle to prepare the usual potato soup for their families. Thick smoke rose from underneath the branches forcing women to cough relentlessly.

The weather had recently changed. Cold, fall air had arrived, accompanied by a chilly, evening breeze. Everyone was forced to take shelter in their tents sooner than usual. Families huddled together to keep warm and to ward off deadly diseases that would strike during harsh cold weather.

Malik took a long deep breath and looked around. Once again, he felt anxious. His palms started to get clammy and his heart began to beat faster and faster. He watched as the small oil lanterns were getting lit in some neighboring tents. They looked like eyes of a ghost in the darkness of the ruins. They looked very ominous to Malik and his hair stood up on the back of his neck. He quickly said a prayer and picked up the oil lamp he usually kept just inside his tent's plastic door.

He lit the little ribbon sticking out of the lamp and placed the smoke-stained glass cover on top. As the lamp came to life, its flicker danced and swayed from side to side. He thought the flame was trying to glimpse at him through the smoke-stained lantern.

He quickly bent down, said another quiet prayer and entered his dark tent. As the light of the lamp pierced through the tent's darkness, his eyes suddenly became cloudy with tears welling up in his eyes. His thoughts went back to his village when he still had a family.

"Salaam (greetings) mother. Salaam father. Salaam everyone." Malik said. But no one greeted him back. The faint light of the lamp did not reveal any faces, and the silence was not broken by anyone's voice. His tent was empty. There was only a thin, worn out mattress lying in the corner.

In the opposite corner, there was a knapsack along with a couple of plates that were cut out of discarded oil tins. He slowly approached the knapsack and unwrapped it with great caution, as to not disturb the contents inside. The pieces of naan appeared hard and moldy, but he kept them nonetheless. Perhaps hoping against hope his parents and little sister would suddenly arrive. Malik wrapped up the naan with great care and laid down on his mattress.

He stared at the sky through the jittery plastic tarp above his head. The sky was clear, decorated with thousands of stars and not a cloud in sight. The wind had blown away all the clouds from the area. The worn out, chalky texture of the tarp gave the illusion of looking at the stars through a thin ivory veil. "Just like Mother's chador she used to cover her face from strange men", mumbled Malik. She was beautiful. As beautiful as those stars. No, as beautiful as the moon. His vision got distorted once again and tears welled up in his eyes.

Slowly, the stars turned into a blurry mess. They appeared hidden behind a thick layer of smoke, the kind of smoke that had engulfed his village following the bombing.

He remembered his father shouting for him to run and not to look back. He had taken off running in front of his father who was holding his baby sister in one arm, grabbing his mother's hand while dragging her behind him. That was the last time Mailk had seen them together. After a series of explosions, Malik and the rest of the horrified villagers ran toward the mountains. He eventually stopped and turned around to make sure his parents were behind him, but all he could see from far away were bodies of people, lying lifeless on the ground, drenched in blood and covered by smoke and mud.

He remembered trying to run back to them to make sure they were not his parents. He had started to run towards them, but someone grabbed his arm very tightly and snarled at him through clenched teeth, "Where are you going? If you run that way, you will be blown into thousand pieces! Don't be stupid now. Keep on running son, or you will get yourself killed!" The man's voice had started to wane. He was obviously afraid.

Malik tried to free his arm from him, kicking and screaming. Then, he cursed and spat at the stranger, but his grip on him never loosened. Malik tried to hold on to anything in his path. As his frail body was being dragged, he tried to grab at bushes, sticks, stones, even dirt, to free himself and not be pulled away from his parents.

"You will get me killed too, you little moron," the man's voice hissed at him now and then. Malik did not care. As he was being pulled away, he dug his nails deep into the dirt, plowing long lines into the earth.

As soon as they reached the mountains and the moment his aching arm was set free, Mailk ran to a far away corner. He screamed like an injured wild animal until he found a huge rock to climb on. Climbing his way up, he kept on screaming like a maniac. Somehow, he did not remember how he managed to get on top of that rock as the rock fell very steep to one side. He recalled seeing his fingers and nails bleeding while he was being dragged. But now he felt the burning pain. He sat on that rock for hours, as the sound of explosions died down. After some time, he stopped crying and screaming. Finally, he remained motionless, as if life had been sucked out from his body.

The villagers began moving toward an unknown destination. They had taken Malik in, and would not let him move far away. They were keeping him close by, just like a herd protecting the little ones from straying. Later, Malik remembered someone saying something to him when he was being pulled from the rock, but his ears were clogged up as if someone had stuffed dirt into them. All he could hear were faint mumblings, lips moving without a sound. But he did not care anyway. If it were up to him, he would continue to sit on that rock until he perished.

Traveling in a world of silence and despair, Malik finally reached the city where everyone began a desperate search to find a corner to live. And he found a small place in the ruins of a schoolhouse.

Six

The sound of footsteps outside the tent startled Malik. He listened intently, as his stomach churned, and his whole body went numb. By now the sound and chaos in the neighboring tents had died down. The usual conversations and voices of men talking about politics and cursing the government for letting them live under such conditions had given way to silence.

How much he despised this silence every night. It always haunted him and allowed the ghosts of the past to invade his small tent. It always tortured him, scared him mercilessly until sleep would come to his rescue and take him far away from his fears.

Malik listened again, it was very quiet outside, and it was late in the night. The weak flame of the lamp had died down too. His heart was pounding very hard. His body felt heavy and frozen. He had heard horror stories of what had happened to orphans in the city. The shoeshines recited daily a lot of those stories, as they sat alongside the Kabul river and waited for customers to arrive. The shoeshines barely looked at their customers' faces. Their job was polishing shoes below by their clients' feet. Eye contact was brief if any cordialities were exchanged. Shoeshines knew that theirs was one of the lowest ranking jobs. They knew they were nobodies in society. Looking at the long row of shoeshines, Malik felt they all looked like dirty rags hanging on the walls of the Kabul river that people used to clean their shoes. "Just a pile of filthy rags", Malik said out loud, as he sat motionless on his small, worn out mattress.

He closed his eyes and began to pray hard. Mid-prayer, he once again heard the shuffling of steps, and then someone stopped by his tent, waiting. His heart began to pound very fast, his body felt hot, and he could hear his heartbeat. He tried to swallow, but his throat was very dry, and it made a strange sound that broke the dreadful silence inside his dark tent. More shuffling noises.

Malik said another prayer and sat on his mattress frozen with fear. He stuck his hand under the mattress and pulled out an old, rusted knife, with a broken tip and half of its handle. *This knife can't even cut a tomato. How will it protect me?* Malik thought as he tried to get up. But his legs felt soft like jelly. His whole body was shaking with fear.

He was too afraid to contemplate what was waiting for him in the darkness, on the other side of the door. The only thing separating him from whatever danger was lurking outside, was a thin black tarp, the entrance side of his makeshift tent. Malik pondered some more. He felt cold sweat trickling down his neck. Finally, he gathered all his courage and yelled at the top of his lungs, "I have a very sharp knife, child stealer! You enter my tent, and I will cut you into a thousand pieces and feed your kidneys and liver to the dogs! You are not going to steal my kidneys or any of my other organs!" His voice started to shake, but he went on yelling, "I know what you are up to. You are not going to knock me out and steal my body parts so you can sell them. If you come in here, I will attack you and bite you like a mad dog! I will scream so loud that everyone comes to my rescue. And by the way, my father should be here anytime, so you better scram, or he will kill you before I get to you myself!" He stopped to catch his breath. He had shouted all this without breathing. At any moment, he expected a dark shadow to lurch into his tent. He squeezed the broken knife very hard and stiffened his fragile body. Suddenly, the voice of a little boy interrupted the horror-filled silence.

"It is just me, Bottle Boy...from earlier. Please don't be angry," pleaded the voice.

The voice trailed off, and once again, there was only silence and darkness. Malik focused and stared into the dark. "There," he whispered to himself, "There they are!" Through the darkness, Malik imagined two strange creatures, hairy monsters with red, glowing eyes. They were standing right across from him, a foot away. The monsters were occupying his space and staring back at him. Then, they smirked at him. They smirked at his blood drained face and appeared to mock him for being so deathly afraid. At once, Malik shook his head several times and opened and closed his eyes. Finally, the monsters vanished back into the darkness and he snapped out of his vision. He felt a sense of relief and eased his tense grip on the knife. *Who is Bottle Boy and why is he here? Could this be a trick*, he wondered.

"What do you want?" Malik shouted, "and why are you here?"

There was a long silence, as he waited for a response from the other side. Finally, the little voice spoke again, very softly, almost in a whisper, "I have nowhere and no one to go to for help. I followed you to your tent here."

Malik sighed with relief. He got up, found the oil lamp and lit it up with a match. After lighting the lamp, he spoke to the yet faceless voice outside his tent, "Come in then and let me see what you look like, Bottle Boy. If you lie or are trying to trick me, you will look like a bottle leaving this tent!" Malik tried his best to sound tough and intimidating. His heart, however, began to beat faster again, as he anticipated facing the owner of the voice that had spoken to him.

A tiny figure entered the tent. As soon as the flame of the oil lamp illuminated his face, Malik recognized him. It was the little boy from the bazaar who was fighting over a plastic water bottle. Malik had stopped the altercation by giving him his bottle. "Oh yeah, I do remember you. But what on earth possessed you to follow me all the way here? Did you think that since I gave you a bottle, I would lead you to a plastic bottle dump? Or maybe, you thought my dad owns a bottle factory? You scared the heck out of me," said Malik with a stronger voice. The fear and anxiety he had felt earlier, turned into anger at the small boy standing in front of him. "What if I had a heart attack?" Malik wiggled his finger at the boy's face. "You do not creep up to people's houses like that!" The little boy tried not to smirk, as Malik uttered the word "houses." Malik noticed the boy's smirk and cleared his throat. "What? Do you think this is funny?" he shouted at the boy.

The boy wiped his runny nose with the back of his dirt-crusted sleeve and began to speak quietly, "Yes…it is a little funny. This is not a house; it is a tent. I just sat outside your tent, that's all. I am…"

But before he could continue, Malik snapped at him, "Now you are going to tell me the difference between a house and a tent? I know very well this is not a house, and I am not blind. My eyes work perfectly fine. I can see your bald head and every grime on your dirty face." The boy quickly wiped his face.

"Alright," said Malik.

"Now that we both know that I am not blind and this is my house tell me why you were prowling in the dark?" But the boy just stared and did not seem to have an answer.

Malik threw his hands up in the air and continued, "God! I tried to do a good deed earlier, and what do I get in return? A heart attack! Now scram and go back home! I have no more junk to give you!"

"But I did not come here for junk," the little boy said. "I have collected enough for today. I have nowhere to go, and I thought I could…"

Malik interrupted him again, "You thought you could do what?"

The little boy looked at Malik nervously. "Stay here …with you," he finally replied. He lowered his eyes staring at his feet. Malik also noticed the boy's toe peeking out of his worn out shoe.

"What? How old are you and where are your parents?" Malik demanded.

"I am six and I got separated from my parents while our village was being bombed. I came here looking for them. I know I can find them one day. This is a big city, and I have to look very hard. But I know I will…," his voice trailed off, as he struggled not to cry. Fighting back the tears, he explained to Malik how he survived each day by collecting and selling junk and sleeping on the sidewalks.

As the boy was telling his story, a calmness came over Malik and he felt more at ease. He listened carefully and intensely to the boy's story. He realized how similar his journey has been. He wondered how many other little boys had experienced the same fate. He thought there must be thousands of boys like him. With so many years of war, there must be many boys and girls like us, Malik decided. He studied the boy again and realized the difference between himself and the boy. The boy still had hope of finding his parents unlike himself who came to an empty tent every night, pretending he was not alone.

"Can I stay here?" the boy's voice startled Malik who had momentarily fallen in deep thought.

"Sure," Malik consented. "I guess. What is your name? I am sure you were not named Bottle Boy by your parents?" Malik smiled. The boy grinned ear to ear. For the first time, Malik noticed that he was missing two front teeth.

"It is Zamaan!" answered the little boy quivering with excitement and relief.

"How about Toothless?" Malik teased him.

The little boy laughed heartily.

"Okay. Here is the deal, you can stay with me as long as it takes for you to locate your parents. It is late now and I have to wake up early to go to work tomorrow. You can sleep in that corner," Malik said, pointing to the far corner of the tent.

After everything was explained and settled, Malik snuffed out the flame of the lamp and once again darkness invaded the tent. Malik looked at the darkness around him and took a deep breath. He noticed that the darkness in his tent did not terrify him like it usually did, he was no longer alone. *I am not alone*, Malik thought. He then listened to Zamaan breathing peacefully. He had already fallen asleep.

I will try to find his parents, Malik made a promise to himself. Once again, Malik started to stare at the stars through the cloudy plastic tarp. He gazed at them as his mind was being flooded with thoughts. Suddenly, many ideas rushed to his head. He noticed a star winking at him.

He smiled and winked back. He whispered very softly, so softly that only he could hear, "I know mother, I promise." He winked again at the flickering star in the night sky. As his eyelids began to feel heavy, he managed to force his eyes open and take another look at that star. Then he fell asleep with a smile.

Seven

The sun rose over the Kabul river. The city slowly came to life. Along with the rising sun, the smells and sounds were resurrected and the layer of dust cast a dark ghostly shadow. The stench of the sewers wrapped itself around each corner and sidewalk of the city and began to taunt every passerby. Pedestrians were rushing toward some unknown destination, appearing lost, worried and already exhausted. The peddlers were slowly steering their unwieldy carts into position. Their carts added to the noise level, making loud creaking sounds, metal grinding against metal, desperate to be oiled.

Once the carts were positioned, the peddlers unpacked the produce and polished them gently with a piece of cloth. And once in a while, peddlers would resort to a bit of spit to get rid of stubborn marks on otherwise perfect-looking produce. This last resort to spitshine produce was, of course, performed as discreetly as possible, such as while bending down and pretending to pick up something hidden behind another cart. Once cleaned, the produce would be organized and displayed with great care and attention.

Due to the number of peddlers, competition was fierce and peddlers did everything in their power to increase their odds at selling. Perfectly glowing apples positioned just right to catch the light, would attract customers and generate business.

Nahim smirked as he sat and leaned against the crumbling wall of the Kabul river. He got ready for the day's work by opening his wooden box and neatly arranging two little bottles of shoe polish along with some old shoe brushes that were missing most of their bristles. Every morning, he was amused to watch others get ready for the day's battle; like soldiers taking position, getting ready for the war of selling vegetables, dried goods, sweets, housewares, clothes and even shoes imported from India.

Nahim often fantasized about owning a pair of those shoes. All he could afford were those shoelaces on them he reminded himself. He derived a lot of pleasure by watching this routine and spectacle every day. That is why he made sure he secured his spot as early in the morning as he could. Every morning, he imagined he was staring at a street scene painted on a huge white canvas which had a beautiful golden frame with intricate designs and etchings, the kind of majestic frame that he had seen while passing by a luxurious furniture store. That store contained enormous frames, all wonderfully crafted and painted. It was obvious to Nahim that only rich folks could afford to buy those frames and that he would never own one. He had observed one frame very carefully, paying attention to its detail, so that he would remember it as vividly as possible. Every morning he would arrange each arriving peddler in various sections and corners of his canvas, filling up the space between the golden frame. Slowly, his canvas would be filled with all the familiar faces and carts.

Eventually, the canvas would get so crowded he could see peddlers pushing each other off the edge of the frame, sometimes kicking and screaming at their rivals just to stay within the border of his spectacularly vivid canvas. He often thought it would be funny if the peddlers fell off the canvas into the dust of the sidewalk. Then, they would all crawl like children to get back inside the canvas and within the golden frame.

Nahim started to laugh out loud. Just the thought of the crabby banana peddler, Zafar, and his long beard, falling off the canvas was too comical.

"Hey, Nahim! Where is your friend today?" asked a shoeshine walking by, interrupting his bemused imagination. "And why are you laughing like a crazy man? What's wrong with you today?" continued the shoeshine. "Been smelling too much shoe polish lately? Has shoe polish been getting to your brain, buddy?"

Nahim, having fully snapped out of his fantasy felt self-conscious. He glanced at the shoeshine in front of him, but had to squint, as the sun was glaring directly into his eyes. He snarled, "No! My brain is in great condition. I have survived the fumes of gunpowder, bombs, fire and above all, your stinking feet, Karim, so I doubt the smell of shoe polish could do any damage to my brain. Since you have been uttering nonsense, it may have affected yours, my friend!" Nahim now stared directly at Karim's eyes. Karim grimaced at him and walked off.

Nahim then quickly scanned the line for other shoeshines, but to his surprise, he did not see Malik. He had been so deep in thought he had not noticed Malik's absence. *He should have been here by now,* he thought. *Where could he be? What is taking him so long? Maybe, he has found a couple of customers on the way here. But that would be very unlikely,* he thought. "He is never late," Nahim uttered out loud, "Why is he so late?" he said again.

"Maybe, foreign soldiers hired him to shine their boots," Karim, the shoeshine that Nahim had spoken with before, shouted from a few feet away. "Maybe, the ones who passed us by yesterday noticed how great Malik was at shining shoes and asked him to shine their boots!"

Everyone within earshot started to laugh at Karim's mockery of Nahim.

"My father says to shine their boots with spit and not waste the polish on them!" said a little boy who was barely seven or eight years old.

"If you do that, they will shine their boots on your face, instead of your filthy shining cloth," roared Karim. "Don't be stupid; you will get us all killed!" Karim finally took his eyes off the small boy, whom he had genuinely frightened with his outburst.

Nobody was laughing anymore; everyone became quiet. Some of the shoeshine kids sitting in line leaned forward and gave the little boy a dirty look. Embarrassed, the little boy froze and just stared at the ground in front of him.

"Where is Malik?" Nahim wondered again out loud. "This is odd; he is never late."

"Maybe he is sick," shouted Karim. "It is getting cold. We will all drop like flies sooner or later," Karim added with a somber tone.

"Or maybe he was kidnapped," said Zafar wearily. "Do you remember the little girl from our neighborhood?" Zafar asked. "Apparently, they stole her kidneys and then left her to die. There are predators around, prowling on little, helpless kids."

"Shut up, Zafar!" Nahim said. "Don't think bad thoughts. Can't you ever begin a sentence with positive thoughts?" Nahim mumbled something else under his breath and gave Zafar an angry look from the corner of his eyes. He also pretended not to be affected by rumors of child abductors that Zafar was alluding to. But deep inside, he felt anxious and apprehensive by each passing minute. His eyes continued to scan the other side of the road, expecting to see Malik walking towards him with his usual gait, his head hung low and shoulders slumped like he was carrying the weight of the world. Nahim sighed and contemplated what to do next.

He suddenly caught a glimpse of his friend Malik on the other side of the road, who seemed transfixed by the chaos of the busy, congested street. The road was filled with honking drivers, some of whom were spitting chewing tobacco out their windows, screaming and scolding other drivers for blocking the road and slowing down traffic.

There were also many cyclists, some with children sitting on the bike's rear seat, or on top of the front handlebar. These cyclists zigzagged between every narrow opening, as the children, with frightened faces, held on for dear life.

Nahim did not take his eyes off Malik and continued to look at him through the thick curtain of dust and haze. Malik was still trying to cross the road and everyone knew that dodging traffic in that section was a risky and dangerous act. Most of the drivers seemed completely oblivious to pedestrians trying to make it alive to the other side of the street. "What? Are you blind or are they invisible?" Nahim would often shout at drivers, whenever he witnessed this battle between cars and pedestrians unraveling. Sometimes, he would see kids who would just close their eyes, scream at the top of their lungs and just run for it. They would make it to the other side, but after being honked at, cursed, scolded, and sometimes even kicked in their butts by angry cyclists. But now, Nahim was relieved and excited to see his friend, Malik, who was still doing the cross-the-road-dance. The dance implied putting one's foot forward, then quickly withdrawing it, and then putting the other foot forward, followed by taking a couple of steps sideways. This dance could be a life saver, even if it looked comical. Nahim felt compelled to say a quiet prayer: "Dear God, thank you. I am eternally grateful to you that he is alive and finally here. I also beg you to save me from the pain and horror of seeing him run over by a car!"

He stood up and waved at Malik in an attempt to navigate his small friend to safety. But his attention was suddenly diverted to a little boy holding Malik's hand. *Maybe that is why Malik is overly cautious today,* Nahim thought. *Who is the boy,* he wondered.

Finally, Malik successfully crossed the road with Zamaan and stood directly in front of Nahim. He was so overwhelmed by curiosity that instead of asking Malik the reason he was so late, he shouted, "Who is he?"

"Salaam," answered Malik. "Oh, this is Zamaan." Malik then continued to introduce the boy to Nahim.

Following the introduction, they sat on the ground and waited for another hour for customers. Malik told Zamaan's story to Nahim with great zeal and passion. He announced that Zamaan would no longer collect junk, but instead, would be in his care until he could find his parents.

Several times, Nahim felt tempted to interrupt Malik, grab him by the shoulders and shake him violently. He wanted to ask Malik if he had gone mad. And how on earth could he take care of someone else, when he barely survived? But each time, he stopped himself. It was because of what he had noticed in Malik that seemed so different that day. That day, Malik had walked up to him with his chin up, something that he had never done before. Also, he noticed Malik talked with a warm smile on his face. And while Malik was talking to him, Nahim saw the little boy, Zamaan, squatting on the ground and looking at Malik with awe. Zamaan would also smile now and then, revealing his missing front teeth.

"Earlier, I told Zamaan …," said Malik, his finger pointing at Zamaan, and the tone of his voice changing to an authoritarian, almost fatherly manner, "You are to sit here beside me until noon and remember the rule, you are to look up at every customer's face, because you never know, he could be your father. And in the afternoon, you are allowed to search the bazaar for your parents, but will have to return here before sunset so we can head home together." Suddenly, Malik paused. He struggled to continue his speech or say another word. The confidence in his demeanor changed and his face was riddled with a sense of doubt and despair. For the first time, Malik realized Zamaan's parents might also not be alive. And if they were, they might not be in Kabul.

Malik paused and thought to himself for a long moment. He finally collected himself and decided he would never mention his doubts to Zamaan. He decided he would never kill that glimmer of hope that brightened Zamaan's otherwise dark and hopeless situation.

Nahim also felt that Malik had come to grasp with the reality of Zamaan's situation. *It was better that way*, he thought. Both Malik and Nahim sat down at the same time. They looked at each other, but they didn't have to say a word. Both knew what the other was thinking. They both acknowledged each other with a slight nod and then leaned against the river's wall. They both looked ahead aimlessly. The expression on their faces made them look much older than they actually were and much more mature. Their faces gave away a sense of resignation to the reality ahead of them. Malik turned his head, and over his shoulder, glanced at the river. He saw dreams, hopes and happiness sink in that riverbed, covered up by garbage, shredded tires and broken plastic utensils. A scream interrupted his dreary thoughts.

"I found it! I found it!" Malik glanced at the source of the commotion and noticed a group of kids dressed in shabby clothing who had, as usual, crawled down to the river bank. A little boy then ran off with excitement, holding a dirty, mud-covered soccer ball. Malik smiled as he watched the kids do a joy dance before climbing up the bank.

"Mr. Rabbit! Are you still dreaming with your eyes wide open?" Nahim asked Malik while elbowing him hard. "From now on, you should only eat carrots! Oh no! My God! Look, your ears are growing longer and getting floppier." Nahim flicked Malik's ears and before Malik could react, he was also flicked hard on the nose! In the blink of an eye, Malik found himself on top of Nahim pinning his arms to the ground. The rest of the shoeshines started to cheer, laugh and clap. Nahim also started to laugh so hard that he could barely speak. All he could manage to utter between giggles was "stop…please…or will …smack …you."

"Hey, anybody up for polishing my shoes?" a voice interrupted the fiasco. Malik could not see the customer as he had his back to him, but his shadow was hovering over Nahim. Malik quickly sprang to his feet, as he brushed the dust off his shirt.

"Yes sir, please place your foot here on the box!" he said attentively. He noticed the man smiling at little Zamaan. Malik's heart dropped and his brush fell from his hand. As he bent down to pick it, he whispered into Zamaan's ear, "Look up, could this be your father?" As he awaited Zamaan's reply, his heart began to pound. The thought of returning alone to an empty, dark tent made him sick to his stomach. Zamaan raised his head to look at the man, but the bright sun made him squint, and he could only see the man's silhouette.

After a few glances, Zamaan looked at Malik and softly whispered, "No." As the man waited, Malik dug a small wooden stick into the shoe polish. He looked up at the sky. He wanted to see if, by any chance, he could locate the star he had smiled at the night before. *I know you are there,* he thought, *even though I can't see you during the day.* He looked at Zamaan and smiled at him reassuringly.

"Don't worry," he said. "I have a promise to keep. Don't give up hope, as our journey together has just started."